Bad Man Love Stories

Bad Man Love Stories

Curtis VanDonkelaar

Etchings Press
University of Indianapolis
Indianapolis, Indiana

This publication is made possible by funding provided by the Shaheen College of Arts and Sciences and the Department of English at the University of Indianapolis. Special thanks to the students who judged, edited, designed, and published this chapbook: Lindsey Henderson, Hope Coleman, Pamela Smith, and Adam Lourenco Fernandes.

UNIVERSITY *of*
INDIANAPOLIS

Published by Etchings Press
1400 E. Hanna Ave.
Indianapolis, Indiana 46227
All rights reserved

etchings.uindy.edu
www.uindy.edu/cas/english

Printed by IngramSpark

Published in the United States of America

ISBN 978-1-955521-02-4
25 24 23 22 21   1 2 3 4 5

Colophon:
The book interior is set with Merriweather
The cover is set in Roboto
and Good Brush (chosen by Adam Lourenco Fernandes)

Cover illustration and design by Pamela Smith
Interior design by Hope Coleman

Table of Contents

An Acceptance

Robbie killed his mother, but I try to think about other things. His floppy sneakers, his t-shirt, with its too-big neck hole, his thin, bony shoulders. He stands in front of me in our kitchen, with something in his hand that he won't let me see, and it's moments like this that I feel particularly ashamed of the things I think and do.

Robbie digs his shoulder into the refrigerator. Behind him, a stack of unwashed dishes dirties in the kitchen sink, and above that, there's a curtainless window. Outside, I can see into the back yard.

There's a split oak and my eventual garden and the last rays of what has been a good day of warm sun. We've just moved, have only lived in this house four days. I should be making dinner, Robbie's probably hungry, but I haven't yet been able to make myself go to the grocery store. Raising a boy alone is hard, hard in the way that hard labor is hard, that chewing rocks is hard.

Dried mud trims the edges of Robbie's shoes like a house's foundation. One of his hands, the right and grimier one, caresses the fridge. The other hand cowers behind his back. Each of his wide eyes floats as a small green bobber on a lake of tears.

"Dad-can-you-fix-him?" he says.

He offers me his hidden hand. Cradled within lies a yard lizard, missing a tail and a left hind foot, its lungs hitching. The lizard doesn't try to escape, tuckered enough by the effort of breath. Spread out across Robbie's palm, its posterior from hips to toes are as flat and distorted as tiny mock-up of a skinned alligator. The lizard drools and its stomach bleeds from an open hole.

"Where did you get him?" I ask.

"Backyard."

Robbie cries two pairs of his stored-up tears. He explores my face, cataloging me as satellites scour the Earth. "It was a brick," he says.

Those patio bricks are heavy. I stacked them beside the garage yesterday, rows of terra cotta squares four high and four deep. They weigh a few pounds each. Robbie was to leave them alone because someday I knew that I would find the energy to stop staring at walls and unswept floors and lay the patio, and because bricks aren't toys.

"I warned you to leave them alone," I say. I mean to be comforting, at first, but the words come out of me like a volley of precisely-aimed arrows. "Those bricks are for the walkway. They cost us a lot money. You don't make enough allowance to buy more if you break them. Not even half enough. You're just a poor little boy."

"They fell," he says. He rubs his eyes before he opens up to me, crying freely. "I saw him, and I reached for him, and they fell."

"You shouldn't have touched them."

"I-dropped-a-brick-on-him-Dad-can-you-fix-him?"

I pinch the lizard between my thumb and forefinger. When I lift him away from Robbie, he doesn't fight. Like a fat pretzel stick, I hold him, flying him through the kitchen air. White liquid drips from his mouth. Pondering him, so like a piece of food, so alive, I squeeze. I squeeze hard, but not even a twitch. I cup his broken body in my own palm.

How could he have not just slid out, come wet and frothy and bawling? He could have, I think, but no. It might be true that my son's head is big enough to be a complication, but that isn't the whole truth. He is a complication. His head's not so big, his rebellion not so small. He resisted, I'm sure of it.

He didn't want. Didn't love the sunshine and the clean air and his mommy wearing that gingham dress. Didn't love her, combing out the tangles of his hair and painting his chest with menthol ointment. Didn't love hugs, scolds over trains left out on stairs, watching him act in a stupid, stupid, little kid play where everyone dresses up like a vegetable.

I lean against the fridge and let myself slide down its front, until I can't slide any more, my back on the white, doubled-paneled door, knees up against my chest. I drop the lizard into the empty space between my feet, where he lies until dead, until he doesn't even gasp.

"No," I say. "I can't."

Facts and Supplications

Franklin, at the dining room table beside Lorraine, tried to move the tablecloth, and she reached across the linen—he thought—to hold his hand. The folded cloth lay diagonally across the hard wood. That was artsy to Franklin. He would've liked the table either fully covered by the cloth, which would have been normal, or fully exposed, because the mahogany was beautifully dark.

"The Earth's core moves faster than the crust," he said. "I read that."

Lorraine caught Franklin's hand and pushed his fingers flat to the table, so that he couldn't move them, or the cloth. Last week, she had accidentally gouged the table with a carving knife. She had to cover the scar so that Franklin wouldn't ever see. She knew this about him: things were better when he didn't know too much.

The sort of thing he would say, Lorraine thought, just as the sort of thing a fly might do was to land on a windowpane and lick its shitty forearms, sit still right in the most visible place, the most carefree spot, where she could smash it with her red-handled swatter.

"Yes," he said.

God, how Franklin hated that flyswatter, how Lorraine would lay it on the dining room table after use, not even wiping it clean. She could take a minute, he believed, to put it away, and not just lay about with death on her hands. He had loved her since the tenth grade, a thousand years ago, but every day of late had been to contract polio, over and over and over. He hoped that someday, they might like to be happy again, but he also liked to dream.

"Yes," he said. "I read that."

And she would, too, just as soon as that stupid meat touched glass.

She frowned.

"What was it yesterday?" she asked. "Something about daydreams and Alzheimer's?"

"The scientists think that daydreaming—" she went on, "—have I got this right?—that daydreaming works a space in your head, the same space where Alzheimer's happens. That daydreaming gives you one of those things, oh what's the word, a predisposition."

"So." Lorraine traced her finger down the tablecloth. She could feel herself getting older. "Don't you wonder, maybe, how they make ships? How they bend the wood? Wouldn't you like to think about that, say, for half an hour? Or better yet, take an hour. I'll go to the store."

"You gotta dream," Franklin said, "in a dirty world. And this one's filthy. Haha, big joke. Turns out, dreams rot your brain."

"Do you want a divorce?" he asked. "Because just say the word."

Franklin had a suspicion that the problem was always Lorraine. Lorraine slapping and pushing at him to think like a dope, Lorraine with her mind a shut-up bodega, Lorraine who never stopped to consider what any one thing meant. She was swimming in all the wrongs between them, Lorraine who balked, and poked, and froze, and who was also an impatient lover.

He nodded. Then he cupped her hand in his own. "I would never. Just so's you know."

"No worse than your planet nonsense."

Spinning hunk of rock, she thought. Melted rock, liquid, like mud. Crust on the outside, a slow-moving layer, a coat of papier-mâché. Lorraine had never played with mud as a child—who would want?—but she felt certain that Franklin had. He wasn't a bad husband, not really, but he wasn't a man at all. He was a small boy, sitting in a patch of wet dirt, eating mud like baker's chocolate, smiling and smearing a cat's thick whiskers onto his face. His mud was just dirt, but he ate nonetheless. He'd eat until the world had nothing but sand-baked glass for skin.

"The word?" she said. "Divorce?"

"No," she said. " I wouldn't dream."

So Moved

A block ahead of the stop sign where I'm idling, a man loads our couch into a moving van. The van's parked in our drive, and the couch is the antique one with the arched back and the clawed feet and the hard ribs beneath a skin of upholstery, the couch my wife brought with her into us, and that she's loved forever— much longer than me—and that we've brought along on each move for the jobs or the kids or the dog or the people we were yet to become, and today, I'm home early, unexpectedly, and she's having the couch moved away, and I'm caught at a four-way behind a man who can't seem to remember which pedal does what, so it's brake and clutch and gas and break and clutch.

Behind the van, boxes of her clothes fill the drive, and the kids' stuff, and even the dog's crate, and I didn't know that we were planning to move today. I didn't call the mover. I didn't know he was coming at all, and it's him I can't look away from. He makes me think of Picasso. The odd, bald man at work in his studio, smoking, at an easel, wearing a smock. He makes the round face of a woman square and the angles of her chair broken.

The mover pauses on the van's inclined ramp and flexes, clenches his hands like a bare-knuckle boxer. He's an inch taller than me and a sack of potatoes heavier, or even two. He channels the Incredible Hulk for one last push, and our couch heaves into the van's open mouth. It's gone.

For good, I'm beginning to wonder.

He loads the last boxes and the dog crate, then tucks up the ramp, and he's gone, too. Our stuff is gone, all of that which was hers, or ours. For good, and here I am, at last at the stop sign on my own.

But no—there's a painter in my passenger seat. He's not a master, just me on the day after we moved in here. This painter, he's about to go inside and explore, run his hand down the jamb of what will become our bedroom door, and he'll get a splinter. Easy to pull free, won't even need a band-aid, but he'll discover there's more work to be done than he thought. Sanding and painting the frames as well. Saturday, maybe. That's when he'll catch everything up, everything that's been left wanting.

But today, I've got another plan. I'm going to make dinner. I'm home early to cook by way of apology. When we were younger, before kids and leg cramps and yearly check-ups requiring us to crush our best parts flat or to let other people send their parts exploring up into ours, we had one good dinner a week. One or the other of us, sneaking home to brew the other's favorite meal.

This afternoon, I'm home early, and I'm thinking about resurrection. I can't get it out of my mind, the image of a man, like me—but no, he isn't—wearing my slacks and navy suitcoat, climbing out of the ground with chunks of dirt between his teeth. He smiles at a woman whispering a prayer before a small pile of stones.

"I'm back," he says. "Did you miss me?"

And she refuses to brush off her knees.

I bought a new roaster on the way, and it occurs to me, if I hadn't stopped to buy the damn thing—if I had stayed instead at my desk and gone on with the giving away of my fingertips for new accounts, a bit of bicep here or there for a bump in sales, all my heart for a new office, one with a view of the parking lot, if I had stayed at work and left all of myself behind, I might have finished the greatest report on quarterly sales increases ever written, and then, fuck that driveway Picasso.

Even now, I'm turning it in. My boss cries over the neatly formatted pages. This is what splendor means. I'm tall and proud, and holding up my chin. I look, like a needy child, into the rheum of his eyes. He rolls the report in his fingers, but he can't open it. The weight of my success overwhelms us both. Look how his hands shake, how his neck wattles. I think, this day, he will never forget.

Larry and Charlene in Three Acts

1.

They planned to try everything short of knives and pliers. The first item would be an executioner's hood. That and two leather harnesses, one for each of them, meant to make things uncomfortable down there. Buying the hood excited them, in theory, in a way that had been missing for some time. Though each had turned fifty-two the previous June, neither Larry nor Charlene had ever been inside an adult bookstore before. Larry felt aroused just walking up to the heavily curtained door. Charlene had to slow her breathing. In, out, she told herself. In and then out, like walking. Full and then empty, her lungs a pair of expanding balloons.

"Perverts, I bet," Larry said, as he reached for the handle. "I shouldn't have worn a good pair of shoes."

"Will they look us in the eyes?" she asked.

A man in a purple dress shirt and a quality tie stood at the counter. He smiled as they passed him. No one else inside. Charlene stopped at a rack of videos, studied one cover. She blushed and said, "Oh my."

Larry found the hood, stuffed it beneath his arm. He found a thong-like G-string with a constricting device on it that he felt he could live with. He motioned to Charlene and she joined him, chose something with a great tangle of straps.

The counter man accepted Larry's credit card, rang them up without blinking. On a six-inch portable television set, the kind powered by D-cell batteries, he watched a syndicated episode of *Divorce Court*. He snorted frequently. As he bagged their merchandise in a brown paper sack, he wished them a good evening.

By the time they got home, the blood had left their groins. By the time they tried things on, they were tired. By the time Larry put on the hood, it seemed so silly to both of them, they stopped and laughed out loud. Larry sat cross-legged in the center of their mattress and Charlene turned on the news. They took off the harnesses, settled into bed for the night. Larry crawled under their chenille bedspread and watched Letterman count something down. He left the hood on.

2.

In high wave conditions, the city of Grand Haven kept the public from driving down to the beach's breakwater by obstructing the waterfront road with construction cones. Larry and Charlene had to drive on the edge of a dune to get around a string of them lined up in a parade of tiny, red-faced dunces. God, if the little fools had only had fingers to wag.

The thunderstorm had another twenty minutes or so to complete its crossing of Lake Michigan, but the storm surge had already come like a slow-moving tsunami, and Larry and Charlene figured they had timed things just right.

Waves higher than their Cherokee broke over the guard rail, slammed onto the street and flooded across it all the way to the far curb. Larry parked as close to the rail as he could. The surging lake was barely the length of a dead man, laid out flat, away from them. Or a woman. Each gush of water rocked the truck as the surf buried them, obliterated their view of the road sign at the end of the breakwater, marked "Danger!!!" in letters redder than the cones.

Larry reached over to the passenger seat and stroked Charlene's thigh. She pulled down the elastic band of her stretch pants, and real, honest, decent effort happened.

He looked up to her. "Well?"

"No," she said. "Not really."

A wave the size of a small house hit them, pushed the truck sideways two feet into the street. For a number of seconds, they floated. The sky darkened, and the first tendrils of Papa Storm rushed ashore.

She said, "I don't think I want to drown."

3.

Larry put his hands around her throat. He could feel her lymph glands, wondered what his life would have been like had he become a doctor. If he pushed hard enough, he could discern the hint of vertebrae.

He squeezed, released, squeezed. From the dresser, the radio played Brahms, the First Symphony. Like a fly buzzing about his head, Larry found the melodies distracting, but Charlene insisted. When they were young, Brahms had never failed to put her in the mood.

"Are you sure you're doing it right?" she asked.

"No," he said.

"I don't think you are."

"Can you breathe?"

"Yeah. I guess so."

They had removed their clothing, done what was necessary for each of them to begin the act. This, especially for Larry, involved recollection. For Larry, of the coed who sold him his morning coffee at Starbucks, her bare belly. His eyes' dream of her bare belly. For Charlene, of the man who came by on Saturdays and offered to rake the lawn for a twenty. Getting ready involved time in separate rooms.

Once they'd officially coupled, he'd clutched her. Afraid, though, to do it for real, he worked his hands as he would have had this been a friendly massage, pressure and then letting up, pressure and good air let through.

"You're supposed to keep going," she said. "Like snakes. They just keep getting tighter."

"I don't hate you," he said.

He had to acknowledge that their sex was already failing. He was growing soft. He could tell that she listened to the music more than she felt him. He considered giving up, but at that instant, she fixed on him and said, "You have to. Do something, do anything."

He squeezed again, this time harder, and he held on a little longer. Charlene turned red, then a light blue. She closed her eyes. When he released, she gasped and sputtered.

"Almost," she said. "Again."

"Will you do me afterwards?"

"Of course," she said. "Why would I not?"

And so he strangled her, hard and without hesitation. She squirmed beneath him, but he only squeezed tighter. Like water through a garden hose, he could feel her coursing blood in his fingers, pumping with her heart.

When she passed out at last, he checked her for a pulse, and then he sat back in the pillows and blankets. Waiting on his turn, he listened to the violins. He studied the play of lamplight on the wall behind the bed. Like a hung tapestry, a swath of bright gold extended upwards from the shade in the shape of an inverted triangle. The light colored the off-white paint against shadows so harshly defined they could have been guidelined on with a ruler and pen. Larry got up on his knees and pressed his not-quite-yet-fat stomach against the headboard. He reached up a hand, laid his palm flat on the unlit wall. A skin of paint, and dear God, so cold.

Moneygreen Buick

Nikki lowered her face to Rick's lap, onto him, and began what he'd asked for. Where her appendix used to be, Nikki could feel the Buick's gearshift pressing insistently, a stitch in her side. Not the gut staples that had held her together in the seventh grade, after the appendectomy, but the pain of running too far, too fast. Then, it had seemed like shooting blanks from her mouth to tell her friends about the operation, to say how it felt to be less an organ: not really that different, not so different at all. The pain had been before; after, the flesh surrounding her scar was numb. When bored, she stroked the scar's ridges, rumpled like a seam of a leather shoe, and even years after, she sometimes noted how rubbery the skin felt. Not human, but animal, as though someone had Frankensteined a cut of pork onto her midriff.

Nikki had begun to disagree with her younger self. Not about her missing piece, but about the importance of speech. Speech kept a person from becoming furniture, she believed, from sitting silent and abused, spilled on, torn up, from becoming an old sofa who belonged by the roadside. *Free to all comers. Free for the taking. Free, Free, Free.*

In her right hand, Nikki cupped Rick's knee beneath the soft fabric of his jeans. Every so often, she scratched the denim threads with her fingernail. By the fabric's feel, dewy-wet and soft, Rick hadn't washed the pants in a week, but she rubbed him anyway, gave him that extra touch of attention. Her left hand tangled Rick's hair, short and mahogany brown, soft like his pants, and easy to pass through her fingers. She liked that about him, that lack of resistance.

He closed his eyes, could no longer see her. She kept silent, had nothing to say.

Nikki wondered—how, would she know, if she were really there? Rick could be imagining her, this, and the sour air that steamed from the paper mill across the street. Men and women inside it moving themselves like pistons, their labor without pause through the night. The neighborhood didn't notice them at night, asleep, and had forgotten how to smell. The possibility struck Nikki that she, her conscious person, this thing she imagined herself to be—unique and skimming the skin of a land called here—this could be figmentary—Nikki, a thought inspired by a coed's bare belly, the smooth, unmarked skin beneath a tie-dye crop top, something Rick had seen earlier at the grocery. She must say a word to know.

Rick breathed in quick gulps, fogging the windshield. Even below the dash, Nikki could smell onions; Rick must've had them for dinner, or at lunch. Certain smells bothered her immensely, especially when they were strong, the sour mill, for example, and onions. Though they didn't make her cry, Nikki thought onions smelled more like garbage than food, like something that should be left buried in the dirt and never eaten. She wouldn't cut them for sandwiches. Boiled cabbage, what Nikki's neighbor made in Crestwood Lanes Apartments, #5A, every Saturday afternoon, salty cabbage broth, an odor that could fill a hallway for a day.

Nikki's mouth, blocked, was full of him. There was insufficient room for her to swell within as well, for the words she might say, the sentences she might become; let loose, they would float as kites upon a beach, as parasails. Her words would have real shapes, triangles, red and yellow silk opened into half–moons as teenagers laughed and fell into clear water.

By streetlight beams, Nikki tried to make out writing on the elastic band of Rick's underwear, but inside the car, the light was too dim. Hanes, she thought; it looked like gray bars. Gray bars were Hanes, two thin blue lines were Fruit of the Loom, and those were by far, in Nikki's experience, the two most common brands of men's briefs. Rick's zipper glinted as he arched against the seat.

Beside her head, Nikki could hear his wristwatch, ticking away. He wore it upside down, the face on the band of skin that a person slashed in suicide, and that meant, as Rick held her head, that the watch hung at her left ear. His was a loud watch, and Nikki had good hearing.

Often, Nikki felt silly for not wearing a watch of her own. If she could find one that she could stand to see in daylight, maybe a simple, black leather band, she could look at it in moments like these, which she felt sure would lengthen out into the golden years of her life. If old age is golden, what did that make her thirty-one? Silver maybe, bronze at least. She was working her way up the podium by the second in Rick's dusty Skylark, her, this thing of her, called Nikki, called other things by men like Rick, this thing with so many other things inside a husk of thingness. She would die here, before ever existing.

His hand was heavy on her head, more than she would've liked. He pressed her further down than was really comfortable, and though she'd never been a gagger, Nikki didn't want to test herself. She pulled up a bit, and Rick only half-resisted. Soft, easy Rick, like the mild cold sore on Nikki's lower lip, knocked into submission by teething drops.

She needed a lot of hairspray on her thin bob, also wispy, to keep it eye-catchy on windy nights like tonight. Rick's grasping fingers could be breaking her hold, she feared, and afterwards, she'd look like she'd just gotten out of bed. That was almost true, but not quite, and sometimes it was only nuance, only the movements of flowers, between left and right, between love and sex, between here and not.

Oh, Rick mouthed, and the job was suddenly over. Nikki hadn't been expecting, which was rare; usually, she had a feel for this, as though she had these two skills: knowing, and holding. Speech in her mouth, a cloud of hornets, a summer storm.

After a flare-up of annoyance, she decided

to be the opposite of what she felt, to not be here anymore at all, but to be on McLaughlin's Pier, at her grandparents' cottage in Silver Lake, Michigan, where at ten, she had had an appendix. She had loved to dangle from the pier's edge, feeling lost in the moment of gravity before tumbling headlong into a blue that was really clear. She let the thing called anger go away, spill into the water, where it skimmed to the edges to congregate with algae. She had been distracted, thinking about hairspray, and the watch, underwear, and cabbage when she'd left home at six. She had been thinking about the edges of her tongue. How long had it really been? she wondered. Long enough.

Uhn, Rick said, as Nikki sat up and opened the door.

He pulled his wallet from his opened jeans, the shiny zipper still undone, the briefs still basking in streetlight. He tossed over a wrinkled, limp bill, and not even a handshake, as though he didn't want to touch the flesh of her opened fingers. Nikki worked her cheeks, searching for her smile, but she could feel them, the hornets, and how they wanted to nest in his hair, find purchase in the comb-over, stick their hard parts into his skin.

Nikki climbed out, watched as Rick pulled from the curb, slowed for the stop sign at Emerson without trying to make the stop clean. His tailpipe was coming unhooked; she saw it bouncing as he shrank away. Half of what he gave her, she secreted into the wire of her bra, and the rest, she spat onto the pavement at her feet.

Oh, she said. Oh, like midnight thunder, like mountain rain. Like a row of tanks, lumbering. They move rough upon a desert village, now bereft of all aid. Oh like a child's want, strong and forever. And all these things are driven away.

He Would Say

Charlie drove past trees. He drove from September's Carmela and leaves that had already turned. They flashed red, yellow here and there, in spots like tiny suns. A field lay between the trees and the road, Buchanan Avenue. Charlie's was the only car and he drove fast, not caring, unafraid. The air was free of manure. The field's plowed soil appeared like ridges of a line of scar tissue set across the hip of a giant and beautiful woman, but the leaves were beautiful themselves, still clinging to branches. Red leaves, brown leaves, leaves struck with purple and orange.

Yellow is simple, Charlie thought. I don't need fancy words. This wind is cold. Those trees are pretty. I'm happy this road doesn't stink.

They had not lived in a house. Carmela had chosen for them a bungalow. She didn't have a couch, as Charlie would have, but a sofa. Their bedroom, a master suite, and what a fine chartreuse bedspread they had lain across just yesterday, spread-eagled, their legs intertwined like bicycle spokes. He traveled east with the trees, and there, there was the bedspread. He blew through it with the speed of an angry man. Green. Light green.

He followed Buchanan, southernmost of ten streets in town named for unsung Presidents, dead men he didn't know.

Fillmore, Tyler, Pierce.

Charlie thinks of knives when he drives on Pierce, knives and the corn skewers Carmela bought for them at Harding's. Shaped like unshucked cobs, they ended in two ice pick prongs. Carmela pierced the plastic knobs into the ends of her corn so she didn't have to touch the cob and get butter on her fingertips. Charlie wouldn't choose pierce. Stab, he would say.

Taylor, Polk, Garfield.

All of them running west to east, and away.

Harrison, Hayes.

The trees passed, north of here.

Van Buren.

He reached a second field, this one still planted with short, late-season corn, standing meekly like rows of gangly children. There he was, in elementary school, he and the other kids lined up after recess at the school's gothic doors before marching inside. There were his classmates' faces in the husks. Sally Hitchens, who was pale as candle wax. She had gray eyes. She cried as she breathed, daily, and with great necessity. Delbert Reese, who had large ears and second-hand shirts. A temper. Once, as they'd fought, Carmela had called Charlie simpleminded, and he couldn't forget the sound, sharp and cold and very much like a blade.

When he left her, she followed him out to the drive, stared after him as he settled into his car. He said, "You could talk any man out of love."

And here was Carmela. Sculpted woman, frozen on their porch, carved guard in a doorway to a foyer, and fixtures, and two table settings. Her mouth open, her hands pressed flat to her sides. Her weak shoulders melting in straight lines to the ground.

"Oh—" she tried.

But Charlie named it a hallway, and lights, and a pair of forks. Cool wind, happy in the air around his Dodge, happy puffing up like road dust. Charlie loved simple. Trees and kids, and his heavy foot, and everything he knew that was now.

Another Acceptance

Sometimes I can't remember if I'm supposed to like to dance. This is not to say that I don't know, or that I can't know, or couldn't say, but only that I can't be sure when I did and when I didn't, and really, what are you asking anyways? Whether I like to dance is the sort of thing that depends on context, like whether I believe my wife is getting fat, or looking old, or just boring the hell out of me on a Tuesday evening. Different answers, my friend, for different days, and that is another reason why I am a bad, bad man.

If I were stopped on the street, and someone held up a microphone, and had a question for me, "Do you like to dance?" I believe that I would say yes, I do. Emphatically, because it's an easy question, as similar to and as innocuous as "Do you like winter?"

Yes. But only with very little snow. Too much snow is like too much sex. In the end, it's just more cleanup and sore muscles.

"Are you a Virgo?"

I am. Born dead center of the cusps, depending on whose chart you follow. She was, too, if that matters for your annals.

"Do you follow the news of basketball in the off-season?"

Believe me or don't, I would say, but I am a Virgo, and I have always been.

If I were asked how long we lived as a couple, the answer being a year, just over a year, before I found the rock in her breast, sneaking up on me like someone else's small and moving knuckle knuckling me back, and Sarah saying nothing, it's nothing, it's a nevermind—I would think about lying. I would say I have followed basketball all my life. Because not all lies are bad, just as not all children are cute.

"Does your wife like to dance?"

No answer. None of the above. Maybe yes, maybe she humored me, but I won't tell the likes of you. This is the prerogative of a bad man, his privacy kept as close and warm as a fifth sheet of skin. We danced in that house, which, I tell you, is true.

And I do like to dance. I find dancing cathartic. Not in the sense of good, sound psychology, of denial and acceptance, of a solid bowel movement, but of finally getting permission to spin so hard, and so fast, I can be sure it's the world gone out of control, and I'm the only one left in town who's normal, who's standing still, who disapproves of everything said and silent.

God damn if I could only cluck my tongue. It's like bending your tongue, in half, they say, a genetic ability only some of us are born with. And I accept that since I wasn't, I can't.

Bad Man Love Stories

I. Surely This Is how a good love is best made broke:

"You don't do some stupid thing I want," he says, "and I want to rain down on the world like God in His baddest pickup. He comes down from the mountains and He brings His mouth."

"Oh?" she asks, because that's what she does for him.

She's sick, ever and always sicker—a land in itself, wouldn't sickness be? An old world—but today, he thinks they might go into a new and different place. He wants to leave this woman—no, he wants this woman to leave him—sometime before her last thing happens. He wants to feel not too bad about departures. So, then, it's time to lie a little, to stretch, to relax the bonds of truth. That's the kind of man he is, and why he hopes to warn her about himself, to warn her away from him. Today if possible.

"That's just one reason that I'm a bad man," he says. "For you, in particular."

"Why a pickup?" she asks, and blue-black TV light shines mute in her eyes.

They don't make answers to questions like these, which lovers should never be and yet are always asking of each other.

She frowns. "And why the mountains?"

"You might as well ask me why a God."

And, "Oh," she gives back on a whim.

He thinks: Because a gun can miss. Because a fist is slow and crude, and often as not, a fist hits weak. Because His world is full of violent men as a forest is full of trees, and you would do well to beware.

He thinks: A saw kills nothing but the edges of trees, because the bark is all that lives. He was once told so by a friend, a man who owned a tree-pruning shop, which was to say, he owned a few saws and a long van.

He thinks: Because a saw cuts deep, down deep through skin, but still only churns dead wood.

He thinks: Because it's a mouth that hurts you best.

But he doesn't say. He's not *that* kind of man. He only wants to fly. Be an egret upon the lakeshore, aloft, and alone. He only thinks.

And then, she's laughing again. She's reading the newspaper, or it's a website. Whatever. Doesn't matter. The particular of sorts a bad man doesn't care much for.

"Did you know," she asks, "that Halloween will be held on Saturday this year? What an odd little town in which we live! It's Sunday that's All Saint's Eve. It's Sunday! Instead, we'll just make it a Saturday, be damned, all those wandering ghosts. On Sunday, we'll all go to church, trick-tired, sack-filled, keep the Lord's Day for prayer and leftover mallows."

"They're scared," she says. "God competing

with all those dressed-up daughters. Those boys with swords. God scared of a day's competition, ten-thousand waifs in rags. Why not just do it on Sunday? Why not be true?"

"School?" he asks. "Because of school?"

So this evening, the business of asking done, they'll sleep together for at least one more day.

What he doesn't think, though she does: She has always heard the warnings.

That she speeds up in spite of limit signs and the radar detector's persistent beeps. That she keeps on running for takeoff. Silly man, she will be the one who learns to live with the birds. So tonight, she will sleep beside him, for one more day, always for one more day until—

II. Another Reason That He Is a Bad Man flows from one plain fact: nothing's the same about how he loves a woman and the way a chainsaw gets put to use. That mix of hot gas and slick oil, done up in a hollow pan, that pulling, and pulling, until cold parts catch, and that pulling, against other cold and metal parts and then wow.

He means to sing that kind of song. Grow ring upon band around a heart, feeding a heart a pulpy hope. That all the loves he's cut can't help but feel him in them still. A soft and woody tree must always feel the saw. Those sharply turning teeth. A saw cuts through every limb into every wooden breast.

What he doesn't mean: Gash-marks and wounded pith. What he does is a feeling. That something is always gone away. Numb hands, numb arms, and all those numb and broken chests lined up in rows. Dead pines in a dead dell. Those timbered bodies. They wait for birds and bees to make their wings again once the saw's been put to rest.

Oh, Lover: Can you feel him in your gut? I mean numb nerves and jangling muscles. I mean cramps and a sore back. I mean that you will always wake up with aches. This is the song he longs to sing. Of buzz and bite and chuck. This is what you will have, when he has given all he has to give.

You had better go.

III. Because He Thinks that she would do well to buy his memory of two kissing children, because he means to warn, a flashback:

Dutiful as any best friend, a lanky boy carries his fourteen Matchbox Cars across the street to a bad man who's still just a little boy, and still just mostly neutral. He comes over to house that will one day belong to an old man—a bad old man—who values the things he has thrown away more than what he's kept, all his wants, squirreled up in boxes.

Next door to the neutral boy, a smocked girl's hair flies a thousand grasping arms, brown and long, waving to both lanky boy and soon-to-be bad little man as they pace through the deck of cars.

This is the last time they will play all together.

Because when the girl moved to the house beside that bad little man, she took up his heart as a jawbreaker between her teeth. Because a day after the cars, bad little man catches kissing girl and kissing friend behind her house, kissing! Linked up in the bushes like fruit and tree, and then, that bad little man makes raucous tattles to every parent with ears.

Nobody in trouble, though. So funny, say the adults. Puppies in play at love.

Because the bad little man learns through this act of unfaithfulness, done in the face of what can only be the epitome of unfaith—to put love before like—he loses all his companions, even the parents. He knows that the adults can see what he knows: There's a difference inside of some kisses. He sees, too, what they must also know: He's too old now, and a little worse in his fallen heart, a little bad, too old to be innocent, too old to be loved without cause, not ever again.

Once a chap's old enough, he must always earn his loves.

IV. **Alone** in a quiet house with a modest and well-gardened yard, exposed oak beams in a tight living room, and a small, mussed cot set back in a dark nook, an old, bad man reads a novel with no name on its spine, his blackberry eyes set over waffled skin and his lanky bones collected up as eggs in a frayed saddlebag. He sits on a four-cornered box, a box full of toys that the squall of children who no longer live here have forgotten that they had ever loved. Many of the toys are yet alive, but they are all hopelessly broken, beyond repair. If this man is a top, he is spinless, he is piled up on a heap of puppets, he is stowed in that box, that trunk, beneath his own fool stooped back. This is the place where he reads to himself, and where he remembers the sounds of words. Those like Dear, or Love. Like Honey, in the mouth, in the stomach. Like Why. Sometimes, he thinks that even a few words from any one of those last, bad days would do. I don't love you anymore. Or, rather, I hate. Goodbye. Good luck. Don't call. Don't write. He could make of his words cut-and-paste copies, he supposed, of what once was. You silly bastard. You no-good bastard. No love of mine could—ever could—and why would?—

But no.

He's not that bad, not anymore. This life's about forward motions, and he's trying to be a learner again. So back to his book. There must be inside somewhere a cause.

To Send

I am welcome to keep every bit of what we owned between us, but everything else is hers. To her new apartment, I am to send what she's left behind: two shoeboxes of old pictures and a stuffed toy banana, never mind the wedding album. Trash it, toss it, paint its shiny pages over with fantastic shades of ochre and yellow—what colors she doesn't care—just be sure to send all of her old clothes, even the ones at the rear of the hall closet and her three cases of cheap wines from the basement. Do not forget her luggage in the attic, under the Christmas tree and a deflated river raft, so she thinks.

Also to send, to stuff into manila envelopes, to lick and to pinch closed their straightforward, metal butterfly clips, to couch in shipping boxes: four second-hand volumes on learning Spanish, bound with library plastic and Dewey-decimalled spines. A zippered bag of her best CDs, especially the few of them—only a few—which are straight-up Kentucky bluegrass. Her high school ring—it's in the medicine cabinet—though I can keep the other, she says, for whomever is next in line.

She says that I am a fool. That I grab hold of and fasten onto many misbegotten things to keep forever in forever places. I keep rude moments in the kitchen and insults in the yard. False ideas about a morning front porch coffee with the neighbor. I wander through bedroom cobwebs of deceit. All her foibles I've favorited in memory, and then there's my omnipresent sense of never being more wrong than Jesus.

So I send dream:

She runs, down a cobblestone road, European and dusty. Houses on her left tease the border of a river, their windows opened to wet breeze. Laid out to dry, checkered towels skirt windowsills, and also rugs seeking fresh scent, a cloud's breath. Down an alley, a babushka bakes black bread, the bread you drink with vodka, smelling it by ritual before you and drink and bite.

She runs, and chasing her are the *Just Married* streamers of our lives, sewn into loops on the fabric of her clean gown. A set of silverware skips behind her bare heels, and then a blue clay teapot—kilned in Prague on our honeymoon—clatters after our knives. Three vases bouncing, hand-blown glass: tear drop, doughnut, figure eight. They ballet to the rhythm of her steps.

She runs and runs, and I watch her shrink as I float the river, empty fists in my small boat. I have no paddle to slow, no legs to run, should I make for shore. I know, as though prescient, that in America, my shelves are deserts. In legless balance, I float, study summer cotton's muscle, so much it orbits.

Awake, I do not believe enough in this thing, gravity, cannot imagine, moons hounding planet, planets hounding sun.

Acknowledgements

"So Moved"
> *Prime Number Magazine*, Issue 181, October 1, 2020

"Bad Man Love Stories"
> *Thrice Fiction*, Issue No. 21, December 2017

"Larry and Charlene in Three Acts"
> *Storm Cellar*, Vol. V No. 2, Fall 2016

"Another Acceptance"
> *passagesnorth.com*, April 2014

"Facts and Supplications"
> *The Potomac Review*, Issue #53, Fall 2013

"To Send"
> *Vestal Review*, Web Issue 43 (February 2013), Print Issue 41 (March 2013)

"An Acceptance"
> *The Emerson Review*, 40th Anniversary Edition, 2011

"He Would Say"
> *Sierra Nevada Review*, 2010

About Etchings Press

Etchings Press is a student-run publisher at the University of Indianapolis that runs a post-publication award—the Whirling Prize—as well as an annual publication contest for one poetry chapbook, one prose chapbook, and one novella. On occasion, Etchings Press publishes new chapbooks from previous winners. The press is the new home for the Floodgate Poetry Series. For more information about these contests, the Whirling Prize post-publication award, and the Floodgate Poetry Series, please visit etchings.uindy.edu.

Previous winners and publications:

Poetry
2021: *My Mother's Ghost Scrubs the Floor at 2 a.m.*
    by Robert Okaji
2020: *Vaginas Need Air* by Tori Grant Welhouse
2019: *As Lovers Always Do* by Marne Wilson
2018: *In the Herald of Improbable Misfortunes*
    by Robert Campbell
2017: *Uncle Harold's Maxwell House Haggadah*
    by Danny Caine
2016: *Some Animals* by Kelli Allen
2015: *Velocity of Slugs* by Joey Connelly
2014: *Action at a Distance* by Christopher Petruccelli

Prose

2021: *Bad Man Love Stories* by Curtis VanDonkelaar
      (fiction)
2020: *Three in the Morning and You Don't Smoke
      Anymore* by Peter J. Stavros (fiction)
2019: *Dissenting Opinion from the Committee for the
      Beatitudes* by Marc J. Sheehan (fiction)
2018: *The Forsaken* by Chad V. Broughman (fiction)
2017: *Unravelings* by Sarah Cheshire (memoir)
2016: *Pathetic* by Shannon McLeod (essays)
2015: *Ologies* by Chelsea Biondolillo (essays)
2014: *Static: Stories* by Frederick Pelzer (fiction)

Novella

2021: *Miss Alma May Learns to Fight* by Stuart Rose
2020: *Under Black Leaves* by Doug Ramspeck
2019: *Savonne, Not Vonny* by Robin Lee Lovelace
2018: *Edge of the Known Bus Line* by James R. Gapinski
2017: *The Denialist's Almanac of American Plague
      and Pestilence* by Christopher Mohar
2016: *Followers* by Adam Fleming Petty

Chapbooks from Previous Winners

2020: *Fruit Rot* by James R. Gapinski (fiction)
2016: *#LOVESONG* by Chelsea Biondolillo (microessays
      with photos and found text)

Curtis Vandonkelaar's work has won prizes in the *Literal Latte* Short Short Contest, the *Gateway Review*'s Speculative Flash Fiction Contest, and the Press 53 *Prime Number Magazine* Flash Fiction Contest. His stories have appeared in *Fifth Wednesday*, *J Journal*, *Aquifer: The Florida Review Online*, the *Vestal Review*, *Western Humanities Review*, *Hobart*, and *DIAGRAM*, among others, and have been finalists with the *Puerto del Sol* Fiction Contest, *The Laurel Review*'s Midwestern Fiction Contest, *Harpur Palate*'s John Gardner Fiction Contest, the *Tusculum Review* Fiction Contest, *Pulp Literature*'s Hummingbird Prize for Flash Fiction, and *Passages North*'s Neutrino Prize. See curtisvandonkelaar.com for writings and more.

9 781955 521024